CRASH COURSE

101 Stories, Each
101 Words
or Less

James Schmotzer

JRLS Books
Bellingham, Washington

ISBN 979-8-218-79366-1
Library of Congress Control Number 2025919914

Cover design by Kyle J. Schmotzer
Book design and proofreading by Jill Flores

Printed in the United States of America

First Edition

Keep up with Jim Schmotzer:
Substack and Instagram: @jimschmotzer

To Connie

I love that we keep making stories
together each new day.

TABLE OF CONTENTS

ORDINARY TIME

July 2002—March 2020

1

WATCHING LUIS

Luis was a sub-par pitcher, but the luck of being left-handed kept him in the "Bigs." He had retired twenty-six batters, some swinging, some watching, three pitches each. No bat touched the ball. All walked away, none argued a call. The crowd had begun to wonder if this might be the first true perfect game in baseball history.

The twenty-seventh batter waited behind, 0-2. Luis's heart raced between giddiness and terror. The sun and sweat mixed to burn his eyes. He released the ball early. It hung briefly before disappearing into the catcher's glove. The crowd froze, awaiting the umpire's call.

July 2002
Bellingham Weekly, Summer fiction 101
First prize

2

DRIFTING TOWARD TWILIGHT

A cool breeze brushes my face, sunlight hits my eyes. I blink and reach for you. Get up, grab the paper, and fix oatmeal for two. Eat alone, the television newscaster mumbles.

Phone rings. Kids want to take me to dinner and talk. I know what's coming: They love me. Want my best. You've been gone so long. I forget things. Might hurt myself. They're busy. Can't always check in. They've talked to the doctor. Found a nice place. I'd enjoy being with people my own age.

They love me and want what's best.

If you were here, I'd be OK.

July 2005
Bellingham Weekly, Summer fiction 101
Second prize

3

THE END

Weekend home from college at the parents', with that damn dial-up. Ridiculous. Should call it "slogging-on."

Finally. "Friends" count 327. I scroll, very slowly, through the list: high school; high school; old girlfriend; college; soccer; cousin; college; high school; high school; Sandy's mom; high school; high school; high school; teacher; summer job; roommate; high school; who's that? ...

Status update: "What are you doing now?" Wouldn't you like to know? "Thanks for nothing." This'll give them something to talk about tomorrow, maybe for a while.

Hit post.

Push up my sleeve. Grip the blade, take a deep breath, and begin the ending.

March 2009

4

HUNTING

Daddy'd wake me early. It'd be dark, quiet, cold, and rainy outside. I'd carry my rifle and hurry to keep up. We'd share cold biscuits. 'Bout the time we got to his meadow spot, the sun would be showing its morning face, helping warm me up. We'd hide, silent, waiting. My shooting was more likely to scare things off than kill them. But Momma was so proud when we'd bring home something I'd shot.

Now, damp and cold, I hold my rifle and wait for a stray Yank. If I get one, my momma and Captain will be so proud.

March 2009

5

CONVERSION

Hell's terror, my sinful complicity (whatever that was) and the saving love of God. All told with flimsy Bible figures on dingy, flannel-covered cardboard.

Fear, or maybe hope, churned in my gut. I raised my hand, was taken aside. I leaned in to listen as the kindly old lady's warm breath puffed on my face. I made a choice, the right one, to ask Jesus into my heart, then followed her lead repeating "the prayer."

"How do you feel?" she asked. "Different? Better? Can you tell God is near?"

"Nope," I answered. "Feels about the same as all other times."

April 2009

6

THE FIGHT

My knees pin his arms. "Give up."

"Let go and I'll kill you." More spit than words.

I land one on his cheek. "Just quit." I'm desperate, begging.

He's focused, hateful, determined. "Never."

I've no fight left but fear revenge. My last feeble swing drags across his nose. Blood trickles. More threats. I jump, run. He's so close. I feel him grab at my shirt. I round the corner, desperately lunge, slam the door, turn the lock. I gasp.

He pounds the hollow wood, screaming, promises my demise.

Shaking, I sit on the toilet praying for our parents to get home.

April 2009

7

AGAIN

Attempt suicide and they put you in the state hospital. Escape (more like sneaking out and crossing the state line), and they let you go.

It worked perfectly. Almost thirty years of obligations and expectations, done. Downed some pills and enough liquor to pass out and panic the wife. Lights, sirens, and paramedics swarmed the house.

Couple of nights and it was all behind him: the nagging wife, spoiled kids, dead-end job with that idiot boss.

All of it, gone. He held the holy grail of a clean slate. It was perfect.

So perfect, he met someone new and got married.

April 2009

8

LET ME GO

It was brutal. Rec league for guys under six feet. Ball-hogging little guards with egos bigger than Wilt.

Game's bleeding to an end. The foul-fest has us playing four-on-three. We have them outnumbered, we're gonna lose.

I'd give anything to be on the bench at the end of this slaughter. One more foul and I'm out. Screw the ball, I dive, going for an opponent's body. He slams to the floor. I dance, giddy, waiting for the blessed whistle.

Ref back-pedals by me, laughing, "Nice try buddy. You're in 'til it's over."

I stayed. We lost.

May 2009

9

FACING MOM

I was thirteen—maybe thirteen and a half—and realized I was taller than Mom. It wasn't saying much to surpass her five feet, but I'd arrived. After I made a smart comment, her hand flashed toward my face. I caught her wrist before she connected. "You're not big enough to do that anymore." My hubris grew with each breath and word.

She looked straight at me, paused, then said, "Do you want me to settle this now, or should I tell your Dad about it later?"

My response was as quick as my release, "Anything you want."

May 2009

10

HOPE THAT WON'T BE QUENCHED

"Let goa' me, girl!" Her stiff arms pushed me away.

"But Momma, Daddy's gone ..."

"Hush, don't cry." Not wasting a glance of her squinty eyes by looking my way.

She soon left, moved to the city. People said there was work there 'cause of the War. I started living with family: aunts, uncles, cousins. Momma's people, then Daddy's. Some I wasn't sure about the relation. Most were nice, but I missed my Daddy and I wanted to go home.

'Bout three years of achin', lost without my family. Heard Momma might be getting married. Maybe they'd come for me. Maybe.

May 2009

11

I SAW IT

I saw it. Tried not to, but it was there. That slight, dark red trickle from nose to lip. Soon she'd taste it and we'd both know. Resignation would overtake us. For so long, we'd hoped and prayed. She'd done all the doctors asked.

We were good people. This wasn't supposed to happen. She was young. Hell, we were young, with kids, jobs, friends, dreams. We knew what they'd say. They'd be so sorry. All treatments were exhausted. They'd do all they could to alleviate the pain.

I looked at my watch, as if it would make a difference.

June 2009

12

TRADITION

Dad made it happen every June 26. He didn't tell anyone why, not even Mom. Told me it was because I was born the day after Christmas. My birthday felt like something of an afterthought, an obligation.

We'd go to a game, majors if possible, minors when necessary. If needed, he'd take the day off. Sometimes we traveled. Even made sure his death didn't break the rhythm. Got sick in August and was gone by Thanksgiving. It's been twenty years.

Now I go with my kids each year. Never told them why. Maybe it's more for him than me.

June 2009

13

HE DIDN'T CARE

She took the kids and left a note. "Don't call. I filed. Get a lawyer." He read it four, maybe five times.

He searched online for local attorneys. Started calling—too late, all closed. Hesitated, phoned his folks. Mom answered. Almost hung up. She invited him for dinner saying, "You shouldn't be alone."

"Maybe tomorrow." Probably not, he thought.

Rummaged through the freezer. Stuck something in the microwave. Turned on ESPN. Burned the hell out of his mouth. Tossed the empty container in the trash.

Couldn't sleep. Went driving. By midnight he was lost. Within an hour, he didn't care.

June 2009

14

HOT SUMMER NIGHT

Sweltering summer evening shifting toward night. Kids playing in the street. Biggest ones wedge open a street drain. Can't move the cover far.

Childish impulse leads to a fire. They scour for stuff to feed the beast. Flames grow and faces glow, crowding to see, dripping sweat into the hole. Someone laughs, grabs a younger child, and holds him over the blistering inferno. "Welcome to hell!" The little guy screams, squirms, and begs for mercy.

Light visible, coming around the corner, reflecting off the eyes of each turned head. Somebody yells, "CAR!" and everyone scatters for the safety of home.

July 2009

15

THE CHOIR

"We really need you. One more guy and we're ready to tour."

"I don't know much about music."

"It's OK. You'll balance the number of guys and girls. A girl in the choir named Susan said I should talk to you. Let me show you where you'll stand. Up here, second row, right of center. Yeah, there. Perfect. Next practice is tomorrow at 4. Can you make it?"

"I guess."

"One last thing. Just move your lips. I mean, don't sing. Susan told me about your voice. But we really need you for the look of the group. See you tomorrow."

July 2009

16

BE CAREFUL

Car barely missed the mailbox. Took forever to get into the house. Flopped into a chair, mumbling.

"Can I help you to bed?" Silence.

She wrapped her arms around him and with a quick lift, forced him to the floor. He groaned. She kicked him hard, in the face and stomach. Too many to count. Finally exhausted, she dragged him to bed.

Next morning, he gently touched his aches, trying to reconstruct the cause. "Hell of a fight last night. Never going back there," he said as he struggled into a chair.

"Sorry, honey. I keep telling you to be careful."

July 2009

17

PEACEFUL WINDS

We spent summers at Peaceful Winds in Florida. One morning, as we left for miniature golf, I asked, "Grandpa, why's the flag only halfway up that pole?"

"It's out of respect. When someone dies, we lower it for a day."

"But, Grandpa, it's always like that."

He paused, looking past me. "Older people here … that's the way it goes."

Two days later, the flag was flying high. A party broke out at the clubhouse, a veritable retiree's frenzy.

Before sunset, there were 15 calls to 911. Three deaths. The flag dropped again. As far as I know, it stayed there.

September 2009

18

LIKE AN OLD WESTERN

A humid summer evening, at least by Portland standards. He stands in the neighbor's yard, calling out insults that morph into threats.

The streets have cleared like an old western. Eyes peer out of windows, hoping to see but not be seen. He demands justice for his offended child. Someone must pay. Like a bull anxious to charge, he looks for his enemy. He snorts and paces.

The sun settles behind roofs and trees. Onlookers lose interest and fade away into the night. Darkness overwhelms the neighborhood. He slips home and downs a few before falling asleep on the couch.

September 2009

19

WHEN SHE'S ALONE

Daddy died on a sunny afternoon when she was a child. Not dark and drizzly like you'd expect. Soon after, Momma was gone; not dead, just gone.

Years she can't remember, or doesn't want to. Sure enough, she married young, had kids quickly. When they were off at school, she'd stare out the front window into the unrelenting nothingness. Divorce shattered her fragile, fading hopes.

An eventual second marriage changed little. Alone again, she rocks her days away until after dinner, someone helps her into bed.

She waits until she's sure she's alone and whimpers in the darkness and whispers, "Daddy?"

September 2009

20

STUMPS

Starting a fire in the garage was stupid. I was ten. The flame jumped to a gas can. I remember the heat and the sound of sirens screaming. At the hospital, they told me my legs were stumps.

Strangely, all the misery brings unending attention. Teachers are quick to cut me slack, and my parents regret not being more attentive. I keep hoping some cute girl's sympathy will result in extended benefits. Looks like I can cruise through college and land a cushy career behind a desk.

All in all, it's been worth it. Just don't tell anyone I said that.

September 2009

21

THAT ONE WAS ANSWERED

They said that God loved me and that I should talk to Him. He'd listen and care.

I asked Him to make my grandma better; she died. I wanted Him to help my dad make more money; he got fired. I prayed for Momma to love Daddy better; they divorced. I asked for help with my schoolwork; I failed two classes. I begged for friends and spent the summer alone.

I cried out to God, trying to understand how this stuff works, and waited in unending silence.

Finally, I asked to be left alone. Seems like that prayer was answered.

September 2009

22

EXPECTATIONS

Not what I expected. I was certain it wouldn't happen to me. I've always been sharp, quick-witted. By its nature, this disease should blind me to reality. Ignorance is supposed to be bliss.

Wrong again. It's here and I know it, if I know anything. What do I do? Fake it as long as I can? Back to the doc and seek treatment? Tell someone? Tell everyone?

What if they already know? What if I'm a fool, the last to know? What if they've long been graciously whispering behind my back, kindly letting me live in my dreams?

October 2009

23

BEFORE MIDTERMS

Called a genius, he skipped middle school and breezed through high school. Got straight A's and a perfect SAT score.

At fifteen, he began college at St. Andrew's, a previously religious school, not far from his home. His goofy glasses and greasy hair only overemphasized his inability to fit in. The first week, he missed half his meals and classes, and was often lost somewhere in the library.

Couldn't find his dorm room one Friday night and wandered in the rain. He was taken to the infirmary the next day and diagnosed with pneumonia. He died and was buried before midterms.

October 2009

24

HATRED OWNED MY BROTHER

The divide was as deep and perilous as any I've seen. Hatred owned my brother's soul.

He burned, trying to make our mother pay for the pain she'd sent his way. We never knew what evil drove him to obsessively plot revenge. On Christmas Eve, days after turning eighteen, he announced he was joining the Army and going to war. That holy night was our parents' twenty-fifth wedding anniversary. He knew this was the perfect day for betrayal.

He was almost right, yet it paled compared to the anguish she felt fifteen months later, meeting his flag-draped coffin at the airport.

October 2009

25

THE FALL CHILL

The sun dipped below the horizon; a fall chill filled the kitchen. They stood looking anywhere but at each other. He stood with his back to the empty child's room. She stood near the sink, wishing for dishes to wash or another distraction. The wooden frame of the screen door tapped steadily in the breeze.

She spoke.

"Why?"

"Who knows?"

"You promised."

"We were kids."

"We could try again?"

"Too hard."

Silence drew any remaining life out of the room. It's impossible to know which was hollower: his eyes or her tears. He was out the door. She heard the car.

October 2009

26

MOM COLLECTED STRAYS

My mom collected strays: people, not animals.

We heard unending stories of people we'd never meet and had little interest in.

She befriended the grocery store worker, the "girl" who did her hair, or the police officer who ticketed her last week. We learned not be surprised when she brought someone home.

The kicker happened at my dad's fiftieth birthday party. I asked him about a couple standing near the food. "Some people your mom met. They said they were lonely, so she invited them."

Her singular life purpose was to rescue others from the loneliness that haunted her days.

October 2009

27

LISTENING IN

Writing in a coffee shop and listening to others is my new entertainment.

The cops to my right are pissed. Listening, I determine that they probably went to a class called "How to Control Yourself in Public and Keep Your Name Out of the Paper."

Two tables away, a young couple is somewhere between getting engaged and breaking up. The outcome may depend upon who wins this argument.

The café owner is on the phone, jawing about the outrageous price she pays for coffee.

Eavesdropping is fun until I notice that the guy behind me is reading this over my shoulder.

November 2009

28

IT WAS A JOKE

Two thousand high school kids and assorted staff members mill around the lawn in midday heat. Flashing lights circle from the tops of trucks, bouncing off every available surface. Firefighters race in and out of the building. Administrators huddle, deep in conversation.

Whispered rumors spread through the crowd. "... by the cafeteria ..." "... started in a locker ..." "... flames crawled out of the vents and ignited the wall ..." "... about twenty-five kids still missing ..." "... they're talking arson, probably by students ..."

I hunch my shoulders, circle with my friends. "Geez, guys, it was supposed to be a smoke bomb, a joke. Whose idiot idea was this?"

December 2009

29

HIS EVERYTHING

Small town kids, met at church, high school sweethearts. Their first kiss was the first for both.

Married young. He was drafted, thankfully after the war. Away two years. Kids followed and filled their years.

The empty nest was an adjustment, but they were committed. Anniversaries passed; soon fifty years were behind them.

They felt blessed to miss the unending illnesses that friends encountered. One Easter morning, he heard her cough and gasp. Her body jerked. He forced himself awake, knowing she was gone.

After the service, he said she was his everything.

By Christmas, he'd met and married Beth.

December 2009

30

GRANDMA'S MESSAGE

Everything at Grandma's house had a dingy piece of tape with someone's name on it. Said that's who got it when she died. Changing the tape became a game. Who wanted a picture of dead relatives when a quick switch could get you the TV or stereo?

Grandma got sick and the switching intensified.

After the service, we were at her house eating chicken, trying to avoid the great aunts and their boring stories.

I slipped into the den to see if I got the TV. Found the tape. It said, "Tired of your games. You figure it out. Love, Grandma."

December 2010

31

SISTER SAID SHE'D HELP

I was the new teacher. School was a mile from the interstate. The community was easily fifty years behind the times.

Recess duty and I'm talking with a veteran teacher. We watch two boys playing basketball. One was in seventh grade, the other in eighth. They move in tandem, switching from offense to defense with the turn of the ball. Score is kept but matters little.

She whispers, "They think they're cousins. But they're not. They're brothers. Born too close and their mom couldn't handle it. Sister said she'd help and raise the little one. Never told 'em."

March 2010

32

YOU'RE WASTING MY TIME

The crowd demanded blood: mine. I thought they were my friends. I thought wrong. My thoughts pushed me forward into his rushing fist. I staggered, dizzy. I couldn't quit. I rounded a right, praying to connect.

He grabbed my arm mid-swing and laughed, "Pathetic. You're wasting my time." The adolescent giant had me by eight inches and fifty pounds. His laugh dripped of arrogance.

It was a magic moment. The crowd turned. A rare breath of humanity appeared in teenage boys. They started cheering for me, not him.

Stunned, he looked at the crowd, then bolted into the darkness.

March 2010

33

HOW TIMES HAVE CHANGED

One drizzly 1921 morning, she sailed for the tip of South America. He left the West Coast for Japan a few weeks later. They left knowing that they wouldn't see each other for five years. No rendezvous in Hawaii, just because. No plane trips home for a sibling's wedding or grandparent's funeral. No phones or internet.

Letters would take weeks on the journey across the sea. That was all they had. That and memories and commitment. They'd write, send, and wait. Letters would cross; their stories lost sequence.

Tenacious hearts endured. Five years later, they returned home and married. They'd promised.

March 2010

34

I STILL HATE IT

After years of alcohol and absence, Dad tried making amends by taking us fishing. He'd wake us early on Saturday. The drive to the stream took an hour on erratic mountain roads, guaranteed to make me car sick. We'd park before first light, unload the gear, and hike to "our spot." If we were lucky, we would only suffer a chilly drizzle instead of the usual downpour. Dad was often lost in a zone. We'd run, laugh, and throw rocks into the gurgling, inviting creek.

"Knock it off! This is serious business. Shut up, stay put, fish."

I still hate fishing.

March 2010

35

THE LONG WALK

Picked strawberries—that's what you did in the summer at thirteen. Up early to meet the bus—one the schools no longer wanted—with a cranky driver who doubled as field boss.

Spent the day bent over the rows. The weather jumped between blazing sun or pouring rain.

This day the rain came in buckets.

"Can we go home? Please? This is crazy."

"Keep working."

We'd show him who's in charge. "We quit!"

"Okay, start walking."

Five hours later, we'd covered an unknown distance, drenched and exhausted. Only a mile from home, the bus passed us. The driver honked, waved, laughed.

April 2010

36

I LOOKED LIKE HER

They said I looked like Grandma, red hair and all. Named me after her: Sarah Joy. I don't remember her. There's a baby picture with me on her lap. She died of cancer that year. Stories made her out to be perfect.

I rushed home after school and went straight to my room. Dropped on my bed as tears overwhelmed me. Momma knocked and opened the door.

"What's the matter, honey?"

Words gurgled through my crying, "Oh, Momma, I'm pregnant."

"Don't worry about that, dear. How do you think I got here?"

Sixteen and pregnant. Turns out it's a family tradition.

April 2010

37

GUESS WE'LL FIND OUT

At twelve, I was smoking. Same age Dad said he started. By thirteen, I was drinking. Just like Mom. At fourteen, I'd shifted from petty shoplifting to jacking a car. Had my fifteenth birthday while working at the state farm for boys. Sixteenth, too.

At seventeen, I was back home. Mom would look at me and cry. Dad would yell about anything. School was a waste of time. Friends shifted. Can't say why.

Turned eighteen, dropped out, left home, stayed with friends. Did some stuff. The judge says I'm an adult now. Old enough for prison.

Guess we'll find out.

April 2010

38

RESOLUTION

Accepted a call offering a settlement, canceled the court date, ended the work of lawyers and insurance reps.

After long days of waiting, news came from the hospital. She was six, brain damaged.

Her mother wailed as the ambulance left—surrounded by sirens, flashing lights, and confusion. People ran, panicked. A neighbor called for help.

Blood pulsed from her gashed head, pooled in the street. We froze; we'd heard flesh, bone, and steel collide. She was out of sight, I'd prayed, we'd swerved. She'd bolted into the street.

It was dusk; Jack was driving to school.

April 2010

39

RIGHT OVER THE PLATE

I wipe sweat from my forehead. Me, a rookie, looking into the eyes of my childhood hero. My mind races, seconds before the action.

Last game of the season, my first year in "the bigs." Neither team's going anywhere. He was playing when I was in little league. Never faced him before. Sounds like he's done after today. Full count, one chance to put him down … or make his day. Why not? Throw him a fat one. Let him go out with a dinger.

The ball heads toward home, maybe going seventy-five, right over the plate. He swings high.

"Strike three!"

May 2010

40

SHE FOUND HER PEACE

Sitting by the window, she'd seen it all. Rain, in its near unending forms, could come at any time in Oregon. The annual dusting of snow could produce a bitter blizzard once or twice a decade. Without warning, fog could be an early morning surprise as it drifted over the ground with dismal gray days replicated for weeks on end. But there was an occasional bright sunny summer day too.

In the evenings, the moon shined bright as it danced through its phases, creating its own calendar.

She knew her place and found her peace, sitting and watching in silence.

June 2010

41

CLOSURE

He found peace in the steady hum of the machines, practicing lines in his head to get the conversation started.

It was so cliché. They'd never really talked. Now, death was near and they'd have their moment. Time for a real conversation. Things long sensed but never confirmed. This was his chance. A son who wanted his father's approval. He sensed it was getting close.

A new nurse entered the room: shift change. She forced a smile, introduced herself.

"When do you think he'll be able to talk?"

January 2011

42

WE DON'T CARE

Coaching rural junior high basketball. We're an average team, but those Catholics—they usually beat us by thirty points—forty-three when we visited their place.

At our gym, I tell the guys, "We've got a chance. Go fast, don't sub, okay?"

No one protests. The game starts.

Halftime, we're up seven. Their coach is livid. They have no idea how to play from behind.

Three-point lead after the third, our shooter fouls out.

One minute left and it's tied. Our guys are exhausted. Their coach is red-faced and screaming. We're laughing.

They win by one in overtime. We don't care.

January 2011

43

HOW LONG?

How big could an eighth-grader be? Willie towered over me. He'd been held back twice. Held back, no one flunked anymore. He wasn't trouble, he simply didn't do anything: didn't talk, didn't study, didn't care.

I called his parents and requested a conference. I planned to ask if there were ways we could work together to help improve Willie's grades and prepare him for high school.

His dad showed up a few days later. "How long does Willie have to waste his time here before he can quit and make himself useful on the farm?" he asked.

Got my answer.

February 2011

44

RESURRECTING EASTER

Easter's just Easter: eggs, bunnies, and ham dinner. Preachers rant about resurrection—Catholics and Lutherans make a season of it—but they're not real Christians. At least, I'm sure, the Catholics aren't.

Christmas, that's a real holiday. Every business plays carols and decorates; TV runs unending versions of *A Christmas Carol* and that Charlie Brown show. How could you not be spiritually moved?

If Christians—and I mean real Christians—are going to save Easter, they need some major help. Maybe church leaders should turn this thing over to the business community. We might be able to save it.

February 2011

45

AFRAID OF FINDING OUT

Mom said it was my choice: marriage or college? Said she trusted me to decide.

Right. Just like she said I could date anyone I wanted, or spend the money that Grandma left me to visit Disneyland for Christmas with friends. Said she'd never interfere. She didn't have to; I always knew what she wanted.

I wasn't like my brother. He did what he pleased and lived with the fallout. She'd explode, saying, "You don't really love me." He'd fake remorse and then charm her into forgiveness.

I never trusted it'd work for me and I'm still afraid of finding out.

March 2011

46

SOMEONE ELSE'S STORY

It would be news if it weren't so common. Local kid makes good—until another small business fails. A lifetime of dreams evaporate into legal arguments and red ink. Credit card living bleeds into bankruptcy. Divorce leads to distance from the kids; another typical chapter of this story. Suicidal thoughts fluctuate with counseling appointments and more medication—until the insurance dries up. Next, a boarded-up building, empty house, or body in line at the mission: the one they used to ignore on the drive to work.

But it's a recession. These things happen. They're just supposed to happen to someone else.

In honor of Bellingham's Project Homeless Connect.
March 2011

47

I'M READY

I promised Mom that if she grounded me one more time, I would leave. She never believed me. You gotta understand … a fourth grader can only take so much.

Don't think I'm stupid. I've been preparing. I started planning, saving my allowance, and hiding granola bars—thinking of what to take, where to go.

Parents are meeting with the teacher tonight, getting my grades. I know what's coming. Two weeks of no TV, no games, no friends after school. Study time.

Can't do it. Tomorrow when she sends me to my room after school, it's time for action. I'm ready.

May 2011

48

NOT A BAD START

A real kiss with a real girl. Not Mom, Grandma, or one of those aunts I hardly know.

I wanted to get it right. You only get one first kiss. I mean, a guy could become a hero or mess up and never live it down.

We were walking home together on Tuesday. My hands started sweating. Heck, everything was sweating. I wanted to run but stopped walking instead.

"Becky."

She turned. I lunged, making a smacking sound, almost missing her lips. She started to laugh but smiled. We started walking again, silent.

Not a bad start for a third grader.

June 2011

49

MY BEST STUFF

I'd always wanted to do stand-up. My family was funny. Dad was so quick; his words would be in the next county before the cousins got the joke.

This was my moment. I had an audience—the coveted, captive kind. They were laughing, crying, and choking. Everything I said was killer—even the words I slurred worked.

I used my best stuff: the teenage couple "lost" in the woods; a priest, a pastor, and a rabbi go fishing.

Then she cut me off. "The anesthesia will wear off in a few minutes. You can have visitors in an hour or so."

July 2011

50

BACK OF THE BUS

We giggled and held hands on the bus in fourth grade. Our first dance was at the seventh-grade sock-hop. In tenth grade, I surprised him with a kiss in the library. We said a rushed goodbye on graduation night.

Lost contact until the ten-year reunion, both married with kids. At the twentieth, he sobbed, told me about his divorce.

The thirtieth, I unloaded my grief over my husband's cancer.

The fortieth coincided with our sixth anniversary and I felt like a kid again, holding his hand and dancing.

Duty and habit led me to the fiftieth. Without him, I left early.

July 2011

51

SADIE

Mr. Parker gave us Sadie. She was brown-red with white flecks. Her tail and tongue flapped when she ran. She followed me to school and slept with me every night.

One afternoon, Billy, the biggest kid around, threw a punch at me. Sadie lunged, pressing her teeth on his neck as a deep growl escaped her throat. Billy squirmed loose and took off. I ran home to Mom, bawling, gasping for words of explanation. Sadie was protecting me.

Mom was sitting on my bed, not Sadie, in the morning. "I'm sorry. Dad took her to the pound. She won't be back."

July 2011

52

STRIKING OUT

Porter was a mean somabitch—made Cobb look like a choir boy. Put two in the hospital: one 'bout died. Prison and Twelve Steps—maybe got religion. Commissioner said one last chance.

Vegas had a line on how long he'd last. By late August, he's flirting with .400. It's baseball—world of redemption and miracles.

Blazing, sweaty Midwest game. He was one for three and up in the eighth. Swung early at first and low at the next. Ump calls the third and was attacked by a flailing bat. Benches froze. Cops wrestled Porter off the field for the last time.

April 2019
Cascadia Weekly, Fiction 101 Contest
Third place

53

THE LAST ENCORE

They crowded the auditorium to see their hero one last time. The former vanguards of radicalism were now retired from corporations and bureaucracies, their bodies failing faster than their idealism. On this night, they were alive again, swaying to music and memories.

Standing onstage was the lone survivor of the '60s band that infused their youthful rebellion. His skills were diminished, voice strained, disdain barely veiled.

The encore was near-perfect as the crowd pulsed forward. Sound overwhelmed the moment, and almost no one heard the gunshot crack, while everyone saw their god drop to the stage.

March 2020
Cascadia Weekly, Fiction 101 contest
Editors' Pick

THE RAGING
(Corona Chronicles)

March—June 2020

54

TOO MUCH PAIN

I always believed in America, God, and country, guaranteed freedom and rights. I trusted my president. He knew what was best and would take care of us. He said, "Don't fear." "Liberate." "Go back to work." My soul raged. Crazy liberals weren't shutting down our country.

COVID-19 infected my husband—fear, hospital, pain and feeling so alone. Then our granddaughter. My secret favorite. Same result, only much more pain.

This is beyond what I can take. I refuse to be next. Thanks for your love and support. I pray my leaving this way doesn't cause you too much pain.

April 2020

55

CAN'T BE

It was a perfect day for a parade.

The organizer, a local restaurant owner, was quoted saying "We're hard-working Americans. We have our rights. We need to work."

Cars, trucks, and tractors were covered in red, white, and blue. They stretched for a mile, slowly making their way through town, honking horns and waving to the cheering crowd.

The crack of the gun was barely audible. Cars abruptly stopped and whispers drifted down the street.

"Someone's been shot."

"A kid."

"Not Amy, she's only three."

"It can't be."

Sirens and lights filled the street as the hushed crowd dispersed.

May 2020

56

OUR SOUL KNOWS

Tuesday bleeds into Wednesday, into Thursday, into Friday—to who knows or cares. Meals morph from a creative endeavor to scouring for palatable sustenance. TV—or more accurately streaming—drifts from overwhelming choices to muddled distractions. Whether shack or castle, home feels too crowded. And the internet just plain sucks.

No matter our "creature comforts" or our sense of control, our soul knows that we do not know what we have always known. Our commitments and connections will wander, bearing the ache and scars long into the future.

May 2020

57

ZOOM SCHOOL

"Let's go. Wait, where's Stevie?"

"I told you, teenagers sleep late."

"We've got six people. This chart shows the day in 30-minute increments. Each person has a designated workspace and device. We'll have two breaks to evaluate progress and lunch together at noon."

"Sheesh, the recruiter said I couldn't join the Army without a diploma."

"Why does Acie get the kitchen table and Marq the new iPad?"

"None of my friends have to work more than two hours a day. This sucks."

"Work with me, people. This is the greatest opportunity for family connection we've ever had."

April 2020

58

ENOUGH

Reality TV crews followed the Newtons, drooling for the pain and grief of quarantine life.

Stereotypes were everywhere: Bess—Mom, a cutthroat executive, Jake—the unemployed closeted gay dad, Sammi—the (secretly) pregnant dropout, Drake—the cute, funny son, and Fritzie—the lovable dog.

Week one drew viewers as the family adjusted to being all together, all the time. Ratings jumped in week two as outbursts edged near violence. After episode three, the show was cancelled.

A national critic noted, "It's bad enough we're all living this every day. We don't need it jammed down our throats at night."

May 2020

59

THANKS FOR ASKING

That first week was briefly idyllic—an extended vacation with the welcome absence of oft-repressive obligations. Week two brought a disorienting awareness of the shift in commitments and relationships that long justified my existence. By week three, I was overwhelmed by the contradiction of increasing time and decreasing motivation. The fourth week brought ego bruises, painfully revealing my inability to turn this chaos into some golden opportunity.

By week six, seven, and eight, I had devolved to maintaining basic needs while bargaining with the Almighty for any possible escape.

Thanks for asking. So, how are you handling the quarantine?

August 2020

60

ESSENTIALS?

Trying to be stealthy, I parked in the back and wore a mask. Maybe I should've gone to another store.

Grabbed eggs, milk, and bread—everybody needs those things. Tried to think what else would look good. Dodged a neighbor with a quick corner-aisle redirection move. Dumped random stuff in the cart. Went to the checkout where a college kid worked the register. He couldn't care less about me or what I bought.

$225, shit. Better than being embarrassed by family and friends for violating the governor's orders when I only needed ice cream … you know, essentials. And the beer.

April 2020

COVID-19 HITS HOME

This collection of "Fiction 101" is told from the perspective of six different kids reflecting on life in the daily reality of the coronavirus.

61

1 - TAYLOR

Mom takes care of old folks and Dad works at a farm. I watch the little ones.

It's tough doing schoolwork when my brother and sister are crying, fighting or hungry. I try to keep up, but sometimes the Wi-Fi goes out. Teachers are nice and keep checking in, but I sure miss my friends.

I wish we could get food from school, but my parents are always working. I have to fix dinner for everyone every day. Why can't Grandma be with us?

Sometimes I wonder if I'll make it until school starts again.

April 2020

62

2 - SOPHIE

During the virus thing, we're staying at Dad's. Mom works at the hospital, so she's really busy. He lets us sleep late. We eat breakfast and check in with school, do some work, play video games, and chat with friends. Dad focuses on his stuff until we get noisy.

At lunchtime, Dad asks questions to check how we're doing. If we can make him think we're caught up, we get free time. There's not much to do, so we get bored. I sure miss my friends.

Sometimes I wonder if I'll make it until school starts again.

April 2020

63

3 - ASH

Mom's usually working on her computer or texting with friends. Dad keeps yelling on the phone, reminding people he's the boss. At least when they're high, they leave us alone. We're lucky when we get take-out, because neither of them cooks worth shit.

I try doing schoolwork. When I need help from Mom, she's busy with the baby. Dad tells me it's my responsibility. Teachers are nice and keep checking in, but I sure miss my friends.

Sometimes I wonder if I'll make it until school starts again.

April 2020

64

4 - JOSEPH

Dad calls, "Up and ready for breakfast by 7:00." At 7:30, Mom starts with, "Write about three things you learned yesterday." Next, Dad takes a break from his work for math and science. Mom does P.E. before lunch. Then we get 30 minutes on our own—no screens. Next, back to Mom for history. An old movie, if we're lucky.

We do afternoon chores until dinner. Finally, 30 minutes of screen time—hopefully connecting with friends. The day ends with reading time and bed by 9:30.

Sometimes I wonder if I'll make it until school starts again.

April 2020

65

5 - TONY

Dad's trying to teach his third graders while helping me do my middle school stuff. He gets edgy quickly sometimes. Mom's gone a lot for her job at the clinic.

When Mom's home, she gets ticked at Dad because he gets frustrated with me. She says things like, "You're a teacher," or "You need to be more patient," which kinda makes him more frustrated.

By the afternoon, I'm glad we're done with school. I sure miss my friends.

Sometimes I wonder if I'll make it until school starts again.

April 2020

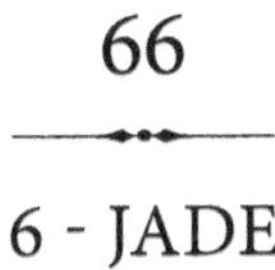

66

6 - JADE

At Mom's house, she bitches about Dad leaving us. At Dad's, we hear about the "assholes that took my job." It's best when he's drunk and not hitting us. We're lucky when they remember to get food on school pick-up days.

I try doing schoolwork each day. When I need help from Mom, she's on her phone. At Dad's, he's usually in his room with his new girlfriend. Teachers are nice and keep checking in, but I sure miss my friends.

Sometimes I wonder if I'll make it until school starts again.

April 2020

67

WE'RE TRYING

"I ... can't ... take ... this ... shit ... anymore!"

"Come on, Kris, language. Your father and I are trying to make the best of these tough times. It's hard on everybody."

"I don't care. I'm outa here. You don't understand. I need some friends."

"You aren't going anywhere. Keys and phone, NOW!"

"But ..."

"Taking away friends and games seems the only way to get you to listen."

"Come on!"

"This isn't a conversation. Take that laptop, go to your room, and get your schoolwork done."

"OK." ... Does she really have no clue what I'm going to be doing all morning?

May 2020

68

THE END OF THE WORLD

It's my 16th birthday, and this quarantine is the end of the world.

Think about it: no driving to school with my new license. No school day with balloons, flowers, somebody bringing me a coffee drink, teachers letting me slide and everybody saying, "Happy Birthday." No ditching campus with friends to get a decent lunch. No Starbucks runs after school. No party with my best friends. No staying out late with my boyfriend and not getting in trouble with my parents because it's my birthday.

Like I said, it's the end of the world.

June 2020

69

LONG BEFORE

My grandma—your great-great grandma— she told me. About 100 years ago, long before you were born, the virus came, and life shut down. Everybody stayed home, didn't go to work, school, restaurants, or shopping.

She said it wasn't that tough until Grandpa got sick. He was tested, and she prayed that it wasn't the virus. It was. He had to go to the hospital. No visitors, not even Grandma. She got updates saying he was fading, and she knew before the final call arrived.

I can tell you, the sadness of loss never left her.

June 2020

70

NEVER RETURNED

" … sharp knife and cheap booze, maybe drugs. So much blood." The EMT shook his head while transferring the patient to the ER staff.

"But he cut off his own hand?"

"He mumbled something about 'How do you know when the germs are gone?' I think he passed out before he could do more damage. Wouldn't have made it here if his sister hadn't checked in on him."

"I think she's brought him in before. Some mental health thing."

"Sad stuff. She told us he's never really returned from that tour of duty in Afghanistan."

June 2020

71

THE VILLA

Always knew I came to "The Villa" to die. The virus ramped up that reality. We've been designated a hotspot. I want to see my kids and grandkids. They say no one's coming or going.

We fly the clubhouse flag at half-mast when a resident dies. Usually happens once a week. Seems like it's down more than up now.

Schultz started a pool. You pick an hour block each day predicting when someone will die. I made a couple hundred bucks on Tuesday.

Sounds morbid, but wait until you hit this stage. See what you do for fun.

June 2020

72

SURE TAUGHT 'EM

News spread: teenagers had organized a "Black Lives Matter" march. Never before had anything like this happened in this small "Christian" town.

Sunday, about 200 locals walked from the high school toward downtown. Hecklers roared by in big trucks, while others stood on porches and under awnings, many flashing rifles, taunting the teens with "Blue Lives Matter," "USA," and "Go back home." Some stooped to, "Black Lives Don't Matter."

The kids banded together, encouraging and chanting in unison, "Love one another."

As marchers dispersed, an old timer was heard saying, "Sure taught 'em what Christian America is all about."

June 2020

THE OTHER SIDE

June 2020—January 2025

73

RUNNING AWAY

After reading books I ran away to join the circus, couldn't find it anywhere.

I jumped a train headed west to see whatever it was that Greeley promised. Discovered it was long gone and sadly forgotten. Found a Montana ranch, tried to be a cowboy, but it was nothing like TV promised.

Stowing away on a plane was my last hope. Finding myself with hypothermia in an unknown hospital was my crushing disappointment.

I went to college, got a job, married, and had kids—like they said I should. And this is where my story ends.

June 2020

74

CAN I HELP YOU?

"Slow down, Andy. I'm going to help that old lady."

"Can I help you get your groceries in your car?" I ask the frail woman as I step toward her.

"That would be …" Her response ends as she turns to see me.

I take the groceries from her cart and load them in the back seat, then close the door. "I'll put the cart away for you."

"Okay." She turns, struggles getting into her seat, then pulls away.

"Adam, that was so weird," says Andy.

"That was my grandmother. Remember? I told you, my choices make me dead to her."

January 2025

75

TEXT TIME

"No! How many times are we going to have this fight? You can't take that phone to your bedroom at night."

"But everybody else does."

"Well, we aren't like everybody."

"But it's my life."

"You may need to find a new life. And you better have your homework done."

"I hate you! Have your fucking phone."

Phone flies across the room, fortunately landing softly on the couch. Feet stomp and doors slam. Hand reaches far into the back of desk drawer, fishes out a burner phone, and starts texting.

You there? It's me, Drake. Guess I have to use this now.

January 2025

76

FAMILY TIME

I look outside.

It looks the same as it has for the last five days.

It's too cold.

It's too cold to go outside.

It's too cold to go to school.

It's too cold to see friends.

It's even too cold to snow.

Mom asks, rapid-fire: "Do you want to play games? You pick. How about a movie? You could pick that too. We could put on our pajamas, make some popcorn, turn on the fireplace and all pile on the couch and watch together."

Life sucks. I'm stuck in this freezing cold house with my family and nothing to do.

January 2025

77

PERPETUAL STRUGGLE

The agenda looks the same as usual.

Susan is fifteen minutes early, wondering where everybody is and whether she has the right date—as usual.

We all sit in our same places—as usual.

Bart is ten minutes late, spills coffee on the table, and gives the same excuse—as usual.

Morgan starts with the same joke and never veers from his script—as usual.

Monty and Susan argue over the new action items—as usual.

Everybody votes to approve the new action items—as usual.

Everybody approves adjournment and agrees to meet on the same night next month—as usual.

January 2025

78

REMEMBER

The light in the window surprises me. I'm a runner. I always get up early. I look at my watch. It's 7:10. I'll sleep five more minutes.

8:12. Shit. Move. I need to be ready for the race next week. I have to improve my pace. This time I will hit that personal record. Every run makes a difference.

Someone is knocking on the door. What? It's 9:23. The door opens.

"Good morning, Mr. Logan. You worried us a bit when you didn't call for breakfast. I need to get you bathed; your great-grandchildren are coming to visit this afternoon, remember?"

January 2025

79

PRIVILEGE PROBLEMS

Credit card hacked. Not my fault.

The bank won't hold me liable for someone in Texas charging $5,000 for assault rifles from Georgia, or the seven grand for a Michigan family to vacation in the Caribbean. Thankfully, it will cost me nothing.

Except I won't have a card until the new one arrives in seven to ten days. I will not be able to charge anything until these issues are resolved, which will take four to six months. My credit score? In the tank. Supposed to clear in twelve months.

The bank will help me clean this up—no problem.

January 2025

80

ALL FIVE PIECES

"Mom, can I buy five pieces of gum with my nickel?"

"Of course, but make it last."

Pointing through the glass, I say, "I want five. The ones with comics."

"Do you need a bag?"

"I've got pockets." Mom nods approval.

While grocery shopping, Mom meets a friend and gets lost in conversation. Billy stuffs all five pieces in his mouth.

"Your son's face is red and he has pink drool!" notes the friend.

Mom looks and gasps as Billy chokes, falls to the ground, and twitches.

An ambulance soon arrives, but they are too late.

January 2025

81

JUSTICE?

Jury duty. Small town at the edge of the county.

Judge said, "Been years since we had one of these."

Drunk driving charged by a rookie cop. Trial goes through the basics. Lunch at noon at the only diner in town.

Judge hands us the case when we return. Deliberate in an antiquated furnace closet: no chairs, no agreement.

At 3:30, the bailiff states, "Judge says if you don't decide by 4:00, you come back tomorrow."

Somebody says, "Guy said it was raining and foggy. Can't be both." No idea if that's true, but we unanimously vote guilty.

Drive home.

January 2025

82

THE LONG WAY HOME

"That's not my house."

"That's not my house."

"That's not my house."

"Let's make a deal. Tell me when you see your house, okay?"

1974. My first day as a school bus driver, taking first day kindergartners home, driving on unfamiliar country roads, with a student determined to keep me on track. I had a paper map and CB radio for help.

"Okay," he responds.

We passed stretches of pastureland and occasionally, houses. All the other students had gotten off the bus long ago. "Remember, I said to tell me when we see your house."

"Oops! It was way back there."

January 2025

83

NOOOOO!

Henry, a favorite camper, and three staffers approached me—the director—carrying a steel drain cover.

Henry called, "I put my finger in this hole trying to catch a bug and now I can't get it out."

The staff nodded.

Sally said, "Heard you can get a ring off by wrapping a finger tight with twine. It shrinks for a moment."

"Let's try."

Sally found twine, wrapped Henry's finger tight, and pulled it away. Henry's finger slid free.

Cheers erupted.

"What happened?" asked Steve.

Henry demonstrated, "I put my finger in this hole and got stuck."

"Nooooo!" I cried. Too late.

January 2025

84

MOVIE TIME

Saturday, movies, seventh-grade boys. More energy than smarts.

Second time through, boredom sets in. Candy bits start flying.

"Shhh," goes the crowd.

Usher points a flashlight at us, "You guys, come here." With sass and attitude, we make our noisy exit.

Owner meets us in the lobby, "That's it, boys. I don't want to see you for a month."

We giggle and pose, strut out front doors into city light.

I'm chosen to call for a ride. "Hi, Mom. Movie is over. Can you come and get us?"

"Oh yeah. It was a good one. We just got tired of watching."

January 2025

85

A DREAM DAY

Meticulous gardens surround the historic mansion.

The sun is bright, clouds are few, flowers are in full bloom, and their scent fills the air.

The string quartet enhances the mood. Guests are seated. Conversations turn to whispers.

The groom and his party move into place, joining the minister.

One by one, the bridesmaids confidently walk the aisle.

The bride appears, her dress perfect. Smiling, she makes her way through the crowd.

Until a sharp click sounds, causing many to stir. Then water, pulsing from sprinklers.

Screaming, scrambling people are soaked before they can get beyond the spray.

The bride falls, sobbing.

January 2025

86

I UNDERSTAND

First day as a teacher—okay, substitute. A dream fulfilled.

High school math. Bell rings and kids are streaming in.

"Look, a sub!"

"New fish."

"Class, please take your seats."

"You new? Never seen you before."

"This is my first time at your school." Don't let them know it is my first time, ever.

"I understand that this school has a 'no phone' policy, so please put your phones away."

Twenty minutes of negotiations. It's all downhill for me.

I put the assignment on the screen and "hide" at the desk.

Didn't realize how fast a dream can become a nightmare.

January 2025

87

REALITY CHECK

Everybody knows the unwritten rule: you can't show favoritism when coaching your own kid. The implication is that you have to be harder on your kid than any other.

But we all know the reality. There are ways to look tough while making subtle moves to enable junior to shine.

It works until the truth is revealed: your kid can't cut it. You are left with the choice of alienating the other parents and their kids, or telling your child the cold truth.

Or resigning and hoping you can avoid breaking junior's heart and avoid seeing other parents around town.

January 2025

88

JUST THE WAY IT IS

In seeking healthcare coverage for which she was qualified, she was unable to understand the paperwork that gave information to connect with the website to download more paperwork, leading to numerous phone calls and hold times of thirty minutes to an hour—when the calls weren't dropped—then talking with a customer care representative who appreciated her patience and was there to do anything possible to help, but ultimately seem unable to answer her questions.

All while the cancer was able to surmount any obstacle in its quest to miserably diminish her quality of life, resulting in another inevitable death.

January 2025

89

MY WHOLE LIFE

Went to church my whole life. My parents, grandparents, and great-grandparents all went to church. Probably family before them went too. Real church—Baptist church. Sunday morning, Sunday evening, Wednesday prayer meeting, and more.

COVID hit. I started doing the Zoom thing. As the weeks went on, I was multitasking, paying less and less attention. I quit watching.

God did not strike me dead. The world kept turning, the sun kept rising, all within continuing pandemic parameters.

Started going to the park for a walk, watching football, getting together with friends for brunch, safely outdoors.

In-person church restarted. I did not.

January 2025

90

COLLECTING

My first paper route was the small-town weekly. I delivered forty *Outlooks*—thirty-five cents a month for the local scoop.

Rain, snow, burning sun, biting dogs—I delivered.

Collecting was the worst.

"I don't have any money."

"Come back when my wife is here."

"I don't get paid until next week."

I mentioned my frustration at dinner. Dad said, "Get your stuff."

We drove the route, stopped at each delinquent customer. I would go to the door, ask for payment. He stood, all six foot three of him, leaning on the car, smoking.

Everybody paid.

Dad never went with me again.

January 2025

91

DOING MY JOB

Working in the steakhouse was great. Started washing dishes and bussed a few tables. Free meals and tips were great perks at seventeen.

Waitresses had to be twenty-one to serve alcohol. They were adults—so smart and funny. Never quite sure if they were flirting with me. I could hope.

Cooks came and went. Some friendly, some not. One spent too much time in the bar before a shift. He started arguing with servers over orders and escalated to throwing baked potatoes at them out the window.

Owner arrived, cook fired.

I was working with a new cook the next night.

January 2025

92

THE EXPERT

Dad was the general manager of a boat plant, overseeing production and sales.

Each winter, he'd bring the new brochure home, and we would choose the color, size, and power of a new boat—ours for the summer months.

We'd spend evenings and weekends on the Columbia with family and friends.

Skiing became a passion for me and my brother.

While backing his rig down a ramp, the new boat slid off the trailer, fast, and bounced to the water's edge. Fiberglass scratching asphalt was like fingernails on a chalkboard.

"Never tell anyone, especially your mom," was all he said.

January 2025

93

WHAT NOW?

Dad left Mom when she was pregnant with Stevie.

We believed she died of a broken heart. Thankfully, she held on until we were all in our teens.

Jackie, secretly Mom's favorite, was helpful and cautious. At twenty-seven, a drunk driver hit her in a crosswalk.

Tommy was Mr. Energy. We feared his love of adventure and risk would kill him. It was cancer, in his thirties—so painful, so fast.

And Stevie—the military, not war. He drowned in a training exercise accident. Never made it to twenty.

I am the oldest, the most responsible one.

Responsible for what now?

January 2025

94

SHATTERING GLASS

Twilight, summer evening. House was full of adults and kids, all enjoyed an unending potluck.

Adults drank. Conversation was loud, music was louder. Some played cards, others danced. Laughter and a few arguments broke out. The drinking continued.

Kids played chaotic chase and catch games, running around or in and out of the house. You could go in the front door, through the living room, out the back glass slider.

The sound of shattering glass and a screaming child stopped the party. Someone had closed the slider. No one told the kids. Jerry ran through it, full speed. Someone called 911.

January 2025

95

SLIDE AFTER SLIDE

The Sunday missionary presentation was compelling. Slide after slide of white sandy beaches, jungle forests, animals so close and big, and natives—rarely fully dressed—doing native things.

He dreamed of having a pith helmet and a machete, slicing his way through the jungle to be the first to find a tribe that had not yet heard the good news of Jesus. He would be an example of Jesus, preaching and teaching the Bible to meet their needs and save their souls.

After years of education, training, and fundraising, he arrived at a village, got jungle fever, and soon died.

January 2025

96

ONE MISTAKE

Bell rang—last class of the day. First day back from spring vacation.

"Why so tired? You spent the last week in bed."

"Yeah, you had the whole week alone with your new husband."

Our first-year high school teacher had made the one grave mistake. Not that she had gotten married and gone on her honeymoon over spring break, but that she had married a police officer—not a popular choice in the politically charged late sixties.

She started crying, called the office. A few were named to see the principal.

The next day, nothing was said about it, ever again.

January 2025

97

LONG, HARD ROAD

Ran away after the Market Crash. Slim chance they'll be looking for me. One less mouth to feed. Mom will cry; food will stretch further. Keep moving. Trade a couple hours' work for a skimpy meal.

Lonely to the bone—making friends is risky. Tough to get a job, tougher to share so little food. And who can I trust if I ever get any real money?

Camps have a fire as the chill sets in at night, but camps are risky, especially at my age.

Not sure I could find my way home. Not sure they'd take me in.

January 2025

98

SURVIVAL

Spent my life covering up, especially from my parents. Didn't want to disappoint Mom, and didn't want the wrath of my father.

Built my skills: fix it, and if you can't fix it, hide it, and if you can't hide it, replace it. In a few desperate situations, I tried to pass the buck to one of my siblings.

Maybe the situation works and slips by unnoticed. If not, it might buy precious time. And sometimes I can come up with a better solution.

Which is all good and true until, as a new driver, I wrecked the only family car.

January 2025

99

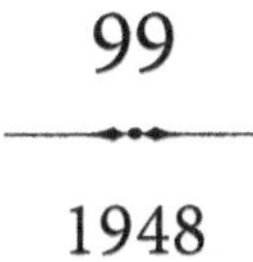

1948

"Make you a deal. You're tired of me, and I'm tired of you."

"You know that's not true, son. We love you."

"Let him talk. We can't keep doing this."

"I dropped out of school. Talked with the Navy recruiter. They say I can go any time. War's over—can't be a hero like my brothers. But I can get out of here. Get a fresh start. I need you to sign this paper. Can't do it myself at seventeen." I hold out the paper and pen.

Dad takes it and signs, gives it back.

"Thanks, good night, and Merry Christmas."

January 2025

100

WHAT YA GOT

The weathercaster was finally right. Deep, white snow drifted around the house, burying cars.

Daisy was dancing at the door. "I got you—let me get some clothes." Snow poured through the open door. "Shit."

Daisy bounded out, darted, looked for the usual grass, gave up, squatted. Her pee leaked bright yellow in the snow. Finished, she bolted toward thick bushes that bordered my backyard.

I gave up trying to ignore her whining. "What you got, girl?" As I approached, I saw something—a body?

No pulse or breath. I called 911, got a blanket. All hope was gone.

January 2025

101

DO THEY KNOW?

Do they know? Do they know I still think about them? Do they know the things I wish I could tell them? To hear and feel their approval, their deep satisfaction in the person I am today.

To reach through that shadow-like veil that, at times, feels like a chasm, and one more time be enveloped in that simple, pure love—love that has more confidence in me than I will ever have in myself.

If they could bridge the mystery, I know they would, and the knowing may be enough to help me make it through another day.

January 2025

ACKNOWLEDGEMENTS

I am thankful for all who have supported me in my writing endeavors over the years.

I am deeply grateful to Mark Nelson, Erik Johnson, Anne Campbell, Bill Palmer, and David Wheeler for encouraging me with this project and in my broader writing life. Each one is a true-life friend.

Thanks to Jill Flores and the staff at Village Books for technical support far beyond my abilities.

I have been privileged to work and volunteer in people-centered organizations and communities for almost sixty years. Every stop on this journey has brought treasured friendships. Many of those continue decades after our time working together.

I am thankful for the deep-rooted love of family. Connie has been a source of grace as days have turned into years, and years into decades. Our sons, Michael, Kyle and Meagan, and grandchildren; Caleb, Morgan, Nevaeh, Kairi, and Atticus bring joy and laughter that daily enrich our lives. My parents, Jim, and Barbara, worked to overcome challenging times and their personal struggles in the1960's parenting John, my brother, and me with love and hope. I miss my parents, and the last of the 101 stories is for them.

Keep up with me:
Substack and Instagram: @jimschmotzer